HOTEL HOT POT OR WHAT

JANE MARRINER

AuthorHouse™ UK
1663 Liberty Drive
Bloomington, IN 47403 USA
www.authorhouse.co.uk
UK TFN: 0800 0148641 (Toll Free inside the UK)
UK Local: 02036 956322 (+44 20 3695 6322 from outside the UK)

This book is printed on acid-free paper.

ISBN: 979-8-8230-8274-7 (sc)
ISBN: 979-8-8230-8275-4 (e)

Library of Congress Control Number: 2023909457

Print information available on the last page.

Published by AuthorHouse 07/26/2023

authorHOUSE

HOTEL HOT POT OR WHAT

Hotel Hot-Pot or What overlooked pretty Wild Flower Meadow.

The attic at the top of the hotel was home to Hatty Bat and her fellow bats who hung from the attic beams. They slept there during the day, swaying gently, as Beau Breeze blew through a hole in the window frame. They also chirped merrily to each other, exchanging the latest gossip. At dusk, they flew into the skies seeking night insects to catch and eat.

Wild Flower Meadow was home to Moogie Mole and his family who dug long, deep tunnels underground, making molehills above.

The large tree in the middle of Wild Flower Meadow housed Maggie Magpie, notable for her love of shiny bits and pieces which she used to line the bottom of her nest.

At the base of the large tree lived Hercules Hare, so called because of his strong back legs. He enjoyed walking on stilts while strumming his out of tune guitar.

Wild Flower Meadow boasted spring snowdrops and bluebells together with summer daises, and buttercups and all kinds of grasses gracefully dancing with Beau Breeze.

One day, Gab and Gabby Grabbitt took over ownership of Hotel Hot-Pot or What.

Gab Grabbitt wore a cravat and a hat at a rakish angle. He liked to tell the hotel guests what he had planned for Hotel Hot-Pot or What.

"Bigger and better, bigger and better!" he told them.

Gabby Grabbitt piled her hair on top of her head, adorned with a large bow. She liked to talk to the guests about the new furnishings and decorations she was planning for Hotel Hot-Pot or What.

Beau Breeze sighed through the hole in the window frame of the attic to Hatty Bat and her friends.

"Gab and Gabby Grabbitt are going to enlarge Hotel Hot-Pot or What. They want to build onto the attic space to make more bedrooms".

"We shall be homeless, where can we go?" chirped Hatty Bat.

Next, Beau Breeze swept down to Wild Flower Meadow.

"Gab and Gabby Grabbitt plan to dig up your Wild Flower Meadow and concrete it over to make extra parking space for more cars." Beau Breeze told them all.

"Terrible news – my tunnels, my tunnels!" cried Moogie Mole.

"Terrible news – my tree and my nest!" cried Maggie Magpie.

"Terrible news – my grassy home gone, gone, gone!" cried Hercules Hare.

"No more lovely wild flowers and nodding grasses!" they all wailed.

"We must frighten people away so they won't want to stay." decided Hercules Hare.

"Frighten away – won't stay!" everyone chanted.

That night, Hatty Bat and her friends perched on the outside bedroom sill of Mr. and Mrs. Grump. The bats chirped and scuffled and scratched as loudly as they could, into the early hours of the morning. Mr. Grump flew out of bed, shaking his fists. Mrs. Grump complained of a headache because she couldn't sleep through the noise. Their little dog charged out of his dog bed, barking shrilly. This woke up all the other guests in Hotel Hot-Pot or What.

"We are never staying here again!" Mr. and Mrs. Grump informed Gab and Gabby Grabbitt.

Moogie Mole and his family loved to dine on earthworms, but didn't think the hotel guests would enjoy them. So, Mother Mole and the baby moles collected as many as they could find. They placed them on large leaves and quietly carried them through the kitchen door at the back of Hotel Hot-Pot or What. It was lunchtime and the guests were seated in the dining room awaiting their lunch. The kitchen tables were covered in salad and meat dishes, and tasty puddings.

Mother Mole and the baby moles waited for the Chef to turn his back. He was busy adjusting his Chef's hat as it had fallen over his eyes.

The moles quickly swarmed over the tables, dropping earthworms into every dish. They then disappeared back through the kitchen door as soundlessly as possible. However, the cheekiest baby mole skipped into the dining room and swiftly dropped an earthworm into the heel of a guest's shoe.

The meal was duly served to the hungry guests, who took one look and rose as one from their chairs.

"Earthworms for lunch, earthworms for lunch!" everyone exclaimed in disbelief.

"We are never staying here again!" the guests told Gab and Gabby Grabbitt, storming out of Hotel Hot-Pot or What. The last to leave, was the lady hobbling outside with the earthworm in the heel of her shoe.

Later that week, a pile of bricks appeared for enlarging the attic space and building new bedroooms.

"What to do now!" cried Hatty Bat and her friends. Then, came a huge cement mixer for cementing the bricks together.

"This won't do" said Beau Breeze, and he summoned his brother winds who were stronger and gustier than himself. Together, they huffed and puffed, raged and roared, until they formed a whirlwind which blew the bricks and the cement mixer far away from Hotel Hot-Pot or What.

Hercules Hare used his stilts to pack the bricks tightly into the cement mixer so that it couldn't be used.

Meanwhile, someone brought a digger into Wild Flower Meadow. Next day, the meadow would be dug over, and a concrete car park laid instead. The Wild Flower Meadow friends gazed in horror at the enormous digger.

Then, Maggie Magpie flew through the open dining room window of the hotel, and picked up as many shiny spoons and forks left unused by the Hotel Hot-Pot or What's guests. She returned to the Wild Flower Meadow with an overflowing beak.

Hercules Hare pulled open the flap to the fuel tank of the digger. Maggie Magpie used the spoons to empty the tank of fuel, and then threw the forks inside the tank to render it useless.

Moogie Mole unearthed the largest stones he could find. Strong Hercules Hare carried them to the mouth of the digger, dropping them inside. Moogie Mole clogged it all up with soil from the molehills.

Next day, the digger men discovered that there was no fuel in the tank, and that it was full of clanking cutlery. They stared unhappily at the mouth of the digger.

"Beyond repair,beyond repair!" they agreed, and trudged out of Wild Flower Meadow.

"Who is spoiling our plans?" wondered Grab Grabbitt.

"We only have one Hotel Hot-Pot or What guest left" moaned Gabby Gabbitt.

That night, Hercules Hare stood on his stilts to reach up to the bedroom of the only guest left in the hotel. As darkness fell, he started to play his tuneless guitar. Miss Lavender Lace had just got into bed. Out she leaped on hearing Hercules Hare's dreadful noise.

"I am never staying here again!" Miss Lavender Lace shrieked, and she fled out of Hotel Hot-Pot or What, still in her nightdress.

The following morning found Gab and Gabby Grabbitt in despair. They knew not who had caused such mayhem.

"Enough is enough", they declared and they packed their bags and hot footed it out of Hotel Hot-Pot or What for good.

There were no new hotel owners after that. Hotel Hot-Pot or What was left in peace and quiet, with Hatty Bat and her friends sleeping comfortably in the attic again.

Wild Flower Meadow was still home to Maggie Magpie and her nest in the large tree.

The wild flowers and grasses flourished, and Beau Breeze continued wafting over everyone with his news.

Hercules Hare still walked on his stilts and played his tuneless guitar.

Moogie Mole and his family made more underground tunnels..

So, all was well once more with Hotel Hot-Pot or What, and Wild Flower Meadow.

Printed in the United States
by Baker & Taylor Publisher Services